Graphic design and illustrations: Zapp

Story adaptation: Robyn Bryant

© 1996 Tormont Publications Inc.
   338 Saint Antoine St. East
   Montreal, Canada H2Y 1A3
   Tel. (514) 954-1441
   Fax (514) 954-5086

Printed in China

THE

*L*ITTLE MERMAID

TORMONT

$\mathscr{O}$nce upon a time, there was a Mermaid named Coraline. She lived in a palace made of coral and shells at the bottom of the sea, with her three sisters and her father, the King of the Ocean.

Coraline had a beautiful singing voice. Even the jelly fish, who usually ignored mermaids, listened to her songs.

Coraline loved her world of peaceful blue water, but she longed to see the sky, the sun, and the moon. "I especially want to see humans," she said. "They must have such interesting lives."

"You may swim to the top of the ocean when you turn fifteen," her father replied. For that was the mermaid custom.

Coraline waited impatiently. Her sisters turned fifteen and made their voyages to the air. "What's it like?" asked Coraline.

They told her about the black rocks and the warm sun. "We saw sea gulls, too. Their cry is very sad. Perhaps they see too many sailors drown," said her sisters.

$\mathcal{F}$inally, the day came for Coraline's visit. She broke through the surface of the foam and smiled up at the sun. Then she perched on a rock to admire the palm trees swaying in the breeze. She had never felt so content.

Just as the sun was about to set, a ship appeared in the distance.

$\mathcal{T}$he ship dropped anchor near Coraline's rock.
  "Happy Birthday, Your Highness," she heard
the sailors shout to the handsome Prince who
was the ship's captain.
  Coraline would have liked to wish him
happy birthday too. But humans were afraid
of mermaids.

$\mathcal{T}$hat evening, there were fireworks to celebrate the Prince's birthday. The party was so noisy that the men didn't hear the wind begin to howl. Soon a raging storm blew up, with fierce black waves.

"Look out!" Coraline screamed, but no one heard her. The ship pitched and tossed, and then it capsized.

*E*veryone was washed overboard, including the Prince. Coraline dove into the water and swam to him. He was unconscious, so she held his head above water all night as the storm raged.

By morning the storm had ended. With the last of her strength, Coraline pushed the Prince onto shore. Then she covered him with her long hair to keep him warm, and sang to him sweetly.

*S*uddenly, a beautiful woman appeared on the beach, and Coraline hid.

"Andre!" the woman cried. "We thought we had lost you forever!"

The Prince opened his eyes. Coraline's song still echoed in his memory. "You have a beautiful voice," he whispered. "Thank you for saving me."

"I didn't save you," the woman said. "But I'm glad I found you."

Coraline returned sadly home. She had fallen in love with the Prince, but she feared she would never see him again.

"What were you doing for so long up there?" her sisters asked. But Coraline was too miserable to speak. For three days, she wept alone in her room.

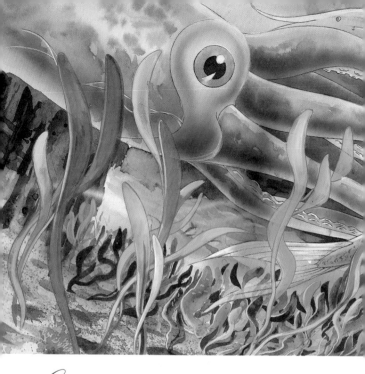

$\mathcal{C}$oraline knew her father would not allow her to return to the human world. At last, she decided her only hope was to visit the Witch of the Ocean.

The Witch of the Ocean lived in a filthy brown bog filled with serpents. She cackled with glee when she saw Coraline.

"So you wish to become human," the Witch said.

"Yes. And I'll do anything you ask," Coraline answered.

"Can you stand the pain of being cut in two? If you take on legs and surrender your tail, that's what it will feel like."

"I'll take any pain if I can walk on dry land," Coraline said.

"In exchange for legs, you will have to give up your pretty voice," the Witch continued. "You will never speak again. And if your young man marries another instead, you can never be a mermaid again, and your life will end."

Coraline nodded quietly, and took the vial of black liquid from the Witch. Then she said goodbye to her watery world, and swam up to the beach by the Prince's palace, where she drank the magic potion.

Suddenly, a searing pain sliced through her tail and she fainted.

Prince Andre was walking on the shore when he discovered the beautiful girl, wearing a most unusual dress of shining scales.

He asked how she came to be there. But Coraline could not answer. Her voice was gone forever. So she smiled instead and leaned on his arm as he led her to the palace.

The ladies of the Court were suspicious of the strange girl. "Look at her dress!" they said. "How did she make it? And her hair hangs in strange waves down to her ankles. Doesn't she know that's dangerous and she might trip?"

"Ridiculous! There are cockle and mussel shells on her toes!" another said.

$\mathcal{B}$ut Prince Andre invited Coraline to stay as his guest for as long as she wished, and the royal court soon grew accustomed to her strange ways. For example, the only food Coraline ate was seaweed salad, which she picked at delicately with her fingers.

$\mathcal{T}$he Prince was extremely kind, and treated Coraline like a little sister. But his thoughts of love were elsewhere.

One day, he told Coraline about the woman who had found him on the beach. "Hers were the first eyes I saw when I came to," he said. "She was only here on a visit, but I miss her."

$\mathscr{A}$fter that, Coraline knew the Prince would never think of marrying her, no matter what her eyes might say to him. She felt so lonely that her heart nearly broke.

"I will stay with him for as long as I can," she decided. But she knew that when he married, she would have to die.

The beautiful woman arrived finally for a state visit. It was obvious that she loved the Prince as much as he loved her.

"Clarisse, meet my sweet little sister, a stranger who cannot speak," the Prince said. "We must always look after her."

When the day came for the Prince to marry, wedding bells rang out through the kingdom. After the ceremony, a great party was held on the Prince's new ship.

Poor Coraline could hardly bear to look at the happy couple. When Prince Andre asked her to dance, he saw that she was troubled. "What's wrong, little sister?" he asked.

Coraline shook her head and smiled as if to say, "Why, nothing at all." Then when no one was looking, she slipped away and climbed into a rowboat. There, no one could see her despair.

$\mathcal{S}$uddenly, from her hiding place, she heard her sisters' voices calling, "Coraline! Coraline!" She rowed quickly out to see them.

"We've come to save you!" they said. "We sold our hair to the Witch for a magic knife. If you kill the Prince before dawn, you can become a mermaid again and come home to us."

Coraline took the knife and waved goodbye. But she knew she would never use it. Instead, she waited until the Prince and his bride were asleep. Then she crept into their bedchamber, and silently kissed their foreheads.

When dawn broke, Coraline tossed the knife overboard. Then, with a last look at the human world, she threw herself into the sea.

Suddenly she felt herself rising upwards, surrounded by Fairies. "We are the Fairies of the Air," they said. "We help humans in trouble. And we take among us only those mermaids who have shown kindness to humans."

So Coraline flew away with the Fairies. And she lives to this day to help young and old who are good at heart.